This most famous of all children's stories was first published in 1908, and its delightful characters of Mole, Rat, Toad and Badger have given pleasure to generation after generation of children ever since. Its author, Kenneth Grahame, was a banker — he was in fact Secretary of the Bank of England for ten years. He died in 1932.

THE WIND IN THE WILLOWS

by Kenneth Grahame

retold for easy reading
by Joan Collins

with illustrations by Martin Aitchison

Ladybird Books Loughborough

1 The River Bank

The Mole had been working very hard all morning, spring-cleaning his little home. There were splashes of whitewash all over his black fur. His back ached and his arms were tired.

It was spring in the world outside. Mole could feel the fresh air and sunshine calling to him in his dark, underground burrow.

Suddenly he threw his brush down.

"Bother!" he said. "Oh, blow!" he said. "Hang spring-cleaning!" He bolted out of the house and scrambled up the steep narrow tunnel which was his front entrance.

He had to scrape and scratch, and scrabble and scrooge with his little paws, muttering to himself all the time, "Up we go! Up we go!" At last — pop! — his snout came out into the sunlight, and he found himself rolling in the warm grass of a great meadow.

4

"This is fine!" he said to himself. "This is better than whitewashing!"

He bounded joyfully across the meadow, till he reached a gap in the hedge, pushing past an elderly rabbit who said "Sixpence for using our private road!" As he crossed the fields, he suddenly came out on the bank of a River.

He had never seen one before. The water was full of life and movement, glints and gleams and sparkles, chatter and bubble. The Mole trotted along beside it, fascinated, until he was tired out.

He sat down on the grassy bank and listened to the sound of the water. As he looked at the opposite bank, he saw a dark hole. Something bright and small twinkled in it. It winked, and he saw it was an eye! Then a small face appeared.

5

A brown little face with whiskers.

Small neat ears and thick silky hair.

It was the Water Rat!

The animals stood and looked at each other.

"Hello, Mole!" said the Water Rat.

"Hello, Rat!" said the Mole.

"Would you like to come over?"

"How can I get to you?" said Mole, not knowing the ways of the River.

The Rat stooped down and unfastened a rope. He hauled up a little blue and white boat, just the size for two animals. He rowed across, and gave Mole his paw, to step down timidly into it.

The two animals made friends at once. Ratty was very surprised to hear that Mole had never been in a boat before.

"There is *nothing* half so much worth doing," he told Mole, "as simply messing about in boats."

Then he had an idea. "Look here, if you've really nothing else to do this morning, why don't we go down the river together and make a long day of it?"

"Let's start at once!" said Mole, settling back happily into the soft cushions.

The Rat fetched a wicker picnic basket. "Shove that under your feet!"

"What's inside?"

"There's cold chicken inside," said Rat, "coldtonguecoldhamcoldbeefpickledonions-saladfrenchbreadcresssandwidges-pottedmeatgingerbeerlemonade —"

"Oh stop!" cried Mole in ecstasy. "This is *too* much!"

"Do you think so?" said Rat, seriously. "It's only what I always take on these little outings."

Rat rowed silently down the river, while Mole took in all the new sights, smells and sounds, and trailed his paw lazily in the water. The Water Rat enjoyed his friend's pleasure and explained why he loved the river so.

"It's my world and I don't want any other."

"But isn't it a bit dull at times?" asked Mole. "Just you and the river, and nobody else?"

"Nobody else! You must be joking! It's full of people — too many of them sometimes — otters, moorhens, ducks and so on, about all day long!"

"What lies over *there*?" asked Mole, waving a paw towards a dark background of woodland, beyond the fields.

"Oh, that's just the Wild Wood. We don't go there much, we Riverbankers."

"Aren't they — very *nice* people in there?" asked Mole nervously.

"Well — the squirrels are all right. The rabbits are a mixed lot. And Badger's all right. Nobody interferes with him. *They'd* better not!"

"Why, who should interfere with him?" asked Mole.

"There *are* others — weasels – and stoats – and foxes and so on. All right in a way. But you can't trust them, and that's a fact."

"And beyond the Wild Wood again? Where it's all blue and dim and there's hills – and something like the smoke from towns?"

"Beyond the Wild Wood comes the Wide World," said Rat, "and that's something that doesn't matter to you or me."

So they began their picnic, and Mole tucked in, for it was a long time since breakfast.

While they were eating, they met two of Rat's friends. One was the Otter, swimming underwater to catch fish. He climbed out on the bank, shook himself, and had a word with them. Drops of water glistened on his whiskers.

The other was Mr Badger, whose stripy head suddenly pushed through the thorny hedge. He grunted, "H'm! Company!" and disappeared.

Mr Toad was on the river, too, the Otter told them. Suddenly he shot past in a brand new racing skiff. He was short and fat, splashing badly, and rolling from side to side.

"He'll never do well in a boat," said Rat.

"Not steady enough," said Otter, and suddenly vanished after a fish. A stream of bubbles on the water was all that could be seen of him.

"Toad's always trying something new," explained Rat. "Last year he had a houseboat. But he soon gets tired of things."

The Rat and the Mole went back to Rat's snug home in the River Bank and sat in armchairs beside a bright fire, chatting away. Rat invited Mole to stay with him for the rest of the summer. The happy Mole went to sleep in a comfy bedroom. His newly-found friend, the River, was lapping against the bank and he could hear the wind, whispering in the willows.

2 The Open Road

Next day the Water Rat took Mole to visit Mr Toad, who lived nearby in a handsome old house called Toad Hall. It was built of mellow red brick and had lawns reaching down to the river. Toad was rather rich, but not a very sensible animal. Ratty and Badger had to keep an eye on him. He was good-natured, but inclined to show off, and he was always getting into trouble.

The friends found him sitting in a deck-chair in the garden, looking at a road map. He had bought a gipsy caravan, painted bright yellow, with green wheels. There was an old grey horse to draw it. Toad was planning his first trip and persuaded Mole and Rat to go along with him.

Toad was bouncing about, full of the joys of the Open Road — its freedom and fresh air. "Here today and somewhere else tomorrow! Across the rolling downs!" he cried excitedly.

The three of them set out, but before they had gone very far, disaster struck!

They were walking along the country lane quite happily, leading the horse. Suddenly a loud POOP! POOP! was heard.

A magnificent motor-car, all plateglass and chromium, flashed past them, flinging out a cloud of blinding dust. Then it was gone, a speck in the distance.

The poor horse was frightened and bolted. The caravan turned over and fell into the ditch. Its windows were smashed and one wheel came off.

13

Ratty and Mole were furious. "You roadhog!" they shouted, shaking their fists. But Toad just sat there in the dust, a dazed look in his eyes, muttering "POOP! POOP!" He did not care about the wrecked caravan. He was already thinking how marvellous it would be to drive a car.

Next day, on the River Bank, everyone was talking about the latest news.

"Have you heard? Toad went up to London by an early train this morning. And he has ordered — what do you think? — a large and very expensive *motor-car*!"

3 The Wild Wood

The long, hot summer had ended at last. Now it was winter. Mole was still staying with Ratty, on the River Bank.

One cold afternoon, the Mole decided to go to the Wild Wood, and visit Mr Badger. He was the only one of Rat's friends that the Mole had not met properly, as he was not very sociable. In the winter most animals stay at home and rest, after an active summer. Some of them go to sleep for most of the time, and you cannot persuade them to do very much.

So Mole knew that if he wanted to see Mr Badger, he would have to call on him.

He slipped out of Ratty's warm parlour into the open air. The sky was steely. The countryside was bare. Twigs crackled under Mole's feet. Trees took on ugly, crouching shapes. The light faded. Mole began to feel frightened.

Then the faces began — little, evil, wedge-shaped faces, looking out of holes, and then vanishing. Mole kept up his pace and, looking round, saw every hole with a face in it, all fixing him with evil, sharp looks.

Then the whistling began. Very faint and shrill, behind, and then ahead of him. Mole was alone, and far from help, and night was closing in.

Then the pattering began. Tiny feet pursuing him, rustling through the fallen leaves. He ran, and started bumping into trees.

Meanwhile, Rat had discovered Mole was not at home. He saw his footprints outside, leading to the Wild Wood. Seizing a stout stick, he set out at a smart pace to track him. At last he found the Mole in the shelter of an old beech tree, trembling all over and so glad his friend had come.

And then it began to snow, thick and fast. Soon a white carpet covered the ground and all the paths and landmarks were lost.

Rat and Mole made their way with difficulty through the Wild Wood. Then Mole fell against something hard, that cut his leg. It was a door-scraper.

"Where there's a door-scraper, there must be a door!" said Ratty sensibly. Digging down, they found a doormat, and then a very solid front door, with a brass plate with "MR BADGER" on it, and an old fashioned bell pull. They tugged at it.

They could hear the bell clanging a long way down. Badger took some time to come to the door, wearing his old slippers and a thick dressing gown. He was rather grumpy at first at being disturbed, but welcomed them in to his firelit kitchen.

Great smoked hams and strings of fat brown onions hung from the rafters overhead. Badger gave them a good supper and they sat talking by the fire, about Toad and his craze for motor-cars. Something would have to be done about that, said Badger, when the winter was over.

In the morning they had porridge for breakfast, with two young hedgehogs who had got lost on their way to school. Badger showed them all the back door out of his lair, through a maze of tunnels that led to the edge of the wood.

Looking back, Mole and Rat saw the Wild Wood, black, threatening and grim, against the snow, and made their way quickly home, safe once more on the friendly River Bank.

4 Home, Sweet Home

It was almost Christmas. Mole and Rat had been out exploring the countryside. It was getting dark when they passed through a country village. Firelight and lamplight shone through the square windowpanes on the dark world outside. They could see children being put to bed, a man knocking out his pipe on the end of a smouldering log, and, in one window, the shadow of a birdcage, with a sleepy bird ruffled up in its feathers. They felt cold and lonely, with tired legs, and far from home.

The two animals plodded on across the fields. Mole was following Rat, his nose to the ground. As he sniffed, he felt a tingle, like an electric shock. Animals can pick up signals from smells that humans never notice. This particular smell meant HOME to Mole.

He had forgotten his own little home in the excitement of his new life. But now it all came back to him, and he called to Ratty to stop.

But Ratty did not hear, and cried, "Oh, come on, Mole, old chap! Don't hang behind! We've a long way to go."

Poor Mole stood alone in the road. He wanted so badly to follow the scent, but he could not desert his friend. He struggled on, slowly.

Presently Ratty noticed how quiet his friend was and how he was dragging his feet. Then he heard a sniff and a stifled sob, and it all came out.

"I know it's only a shabby little place," sobbed Mole, his paw to his eyes, "not like your cosy home, or Toad Hall. But it was my own, and I was fond of it."

Ratty patted his shoulder. "What a selfish pig I've been," he thought. And he turned Mole round and they set off back the way they had come, to pick up the scent.

At last, after several false starts, Mole crossed a ditch, scrambled through a hedge and dived down a tunnel. At the end of it was a little front door with "MOLE END" painted on it. Mole lit a lantern and they could see a neat forecourt, with a garden seat, some hanging baskets with ferns, and a plaster bust of Queen Victoria.

There was a skittle alley, too, with benches and tables, and a goldfish pond with a cockleshell border.

Inside everything was dusty and rather shabby. Mole started to sniff again, ashamed at having brought his friend there. But Ratty ran to and fro, lighting lamps and candles, exploring rooms and cupboards. He started to light a fire, while Mole got busy with a duster.

"What a capital little house this is!" Rat called out cheerfully. "So compact and well planned!"

"But I haven't got anything for supper!" Mole wailed.

"Rubbish!" said the Rat. "I spy a sardine-tin opener, so there must be some sardines." They found some biscuits and were just about to open the sardines, when there was a scuffling noise in the forecourt, a lot of coughing, and a murmur of tiny voices.

"What's that?" asked Rat.

"It must be the fieldmice," answered Mole. "They go round at this time of year, carol-singing."

They opened the door, and there, in the light of a lantern, eight or ten little fieldmice stood in a semi-circle.

They wore red knitted scarves round their necks, and they jigged up and down to keep their feet warm.

"One, two, three!" cried the eldest one, and their shrill tiny voices rose in an old-time carol, about the animals in the stable at Bethlehem.

> "Who were the first to cry Nowell?
> Animals all as it befell,
> In the stable where they did dwell
> Joy shall be theirs in the morning!"

Just as they finished, the sound of distant church bells came floating down the tunnel.

Mole and Rat welcomed the little carol-singers in, and Ratty sent one of them off with a basket, and some money, to buy food. The rest of the mice sat on a bench by the fire and warmed their chilblains, drinking mugs of hot punch. When the messenger returned, they had a splendid supper.

They finally clattered off home, with presents for their families. Mole and Rat tucked themselves into bed in handy sleeping bunks. Before he closed his eyes, Mole looked happily about his old room in the glow of the firelight.

Thanks to the kindness of his friend, Mole's pleasure in his old home had returned. ''Everyone needs a place of their own to come back to,'' he thought drowsily, before he dropped off to sleep.

5 Mr Toad

One bright morning in early summer, Badger kept his promise to visit Ratty and Mole.

''It's time we did something about Toad,'' he grunted. ''He's a disgrace to the neighbourhood. What my old friend, his father, would have said about his doings, I don't like

to think. This craze for motor-cars is getting him into trouble with the police."

"Yes, he's had several crashes," agreed Rat. "I hear he has ordered another new car this week."

They set off for Toad Hall. Sure enough, there at the front door stood a shiny, brand-new, bright red motor-car. Mr Toad, in goggles, cap, gaiters and a huge overcoat, came swaggering down the steps, putting on his big leather driving gloves.

"You're just in time for a jolly spin, you fellows!" he called out cheerfully.

"Oh, no, you don't!" said Badger gruffly, seizing him by the scruff of the neck and marching him back into the house. Mole and Rat took off his ridiculous motoring togs, and Badger gave him a good talking-to.

Toad refused to promise to give up driving, so they locked him in his bedroom to think it over.

But cunning Toad pretended to be ill, and while they were fetching the doctor, he skipped out of the window and bounced off to the village, laughing at his own cleverness and murmuring, ''Poop! Poop!''

In the inn yard he saw a beautiful motor-car, whose owners were inside, having lunch. Toad could not resist trying it out. He turned the starting handle, hopped in behind the wheel, and drove off in a cloud of white dust.

As he sped along he chanted a little song, all about how clever he was.

Toad's next appearance was as a limp and miserable prisoner in the dock at the Magistrates' Court.

He was charged with dangerous driving, stealing a motor-car, and, worst of all, cheeking the police. The Magistrate took a serious view and sentenced him to twenty years' imprisonment.

The wretched Toad was handcuffed and marched across the square to the ancient castle, with its tall towers and grim keep, guarded by men-at-arms, and warders. He was dragged through the arched gateway, and through courtyards where huge bloodhounds strained at their leashes. Down spiral stone staircases he went, passing the rack room and the thumbscrew room, until he reached the deepest dungeon of all. In front of the heavy nail-studded door sat an ancient gaoler with a mighty bunch of keys.

Toad could never hope to get out of there, for it was the best guarded prison in England.

The unhappy Toad realised what a foolish animal he had been.

"What has happened to the clever, popular Mr Toad whom everybody respected?" he whimpered. "O wretched animal, so justly punished!"

He refused all food and lay limply on his bed, fat tears rolling down his flabby cheeks.

6 Toad's Escape

The gaoler's daughter was a kind young girl who was very fond of animals. She took pity on Toad, and coaxed him to eat some hot buttered toast, asking him to tell her all about Toad Hall. Soon the Toad revived a little, and began to puff himself up, and boast about his home and his possessions.

In spite of his conceit, the young girl was sorry for him. She hated to see animals shut up. So she thought of a plan to help him to escape. He was to dress in her aunt's clothes.

Her aunt was a washerwoman, who came to the castle once a week. She was short and stout (like Toad!) She wore a long, cotton dress, a shawl, and an old blue bonnet, and carried a basket full of washing. Toad did not like the idea of dressing up as a poor old woman, but in the end he agreed to pay her some money and tie her up, so that she would not get into trouble for helping him.

The gaoler's daughter giggled as she tied the bonnet strings under Toad's chin.

"You look exactly like her!" she laughed (much to Toad's annoyance.) "Goodbye, and good luck! Be careful what you say to the sentries!"

There were some anxious moments as Toad
set off, especially as the sentries made rude
remarks. But Toad entered into the spirit of
the thing, for he fancied himself as an actor.
Soon he came through the prison gate into the
sunlight and was free at last.

He made for the railway station and was about to buy a ticket, when he realised he had left his waistcoat, with all his money, in his cell. What could he do now? Then he spotted the engine driver, cleaning down his steam engine with a handful of cotton waste.

"Oh, sir," he cried, "I'm a poor washerwoman who's lost her purse. How am I going to get home and what will my little children do without me?"

The kind engine driver said, "Tell you what, missus, I'll give you a ride on my footplate,

and you can wash some shirts for me when you get home."

Toad accepted eagerly and hopped up on the engine. They got up steam and set off. They were soon thudding away down the track, with a trail of white smoke and a whooping whistle.

Suddenly the engine driver looked back. "There's another train following us down the line!" he cried. "It's full of people — policemen with truncheons — plain clothes men with bowler hats and umbrellas — prison warders with sticks — all shouting STOP! STOP! STOP!"

Toad fell on his knees among the coal and begged for help. "I am not a washerwoman at all," he confessed. "I am the well-known daring criminal, Mr Toad. Please help me."

The engine driver hated to see an animal hunted. "Never mind, I'll help you," he said. "When we get through this tunnel, I'll slow down, and you can jump off and hide in the wood."

They piled on more coal to get up speed, and the sparks flew as they roared through the tunnel. Then they slowed down. Toad jumped off, and rolled down the bank into the wood. He laughed as he saw the other train tear past, full of policemen and warders, waving their weapons and shouting "STOP!"

Then he found an old tree, and lay down on a bed of leaves to wait for morning.

7 The Pipes of Pan

Meanwhile, on the River Bank, everyone was worried. Otter's baby son was missing from home. He had never been away so long before. Search parties went out to look for him, but no one could find him anywhere.

Mole and Ratty were very upset.

"Otter is watching by the ford," said Ratty. "It's where he taught him to swim. It was little Portly's favourite place. Otter thought he might come back there. He has been waiting there all night."

It was getting towards dawn when Mole said, "Come on, Rat, I can't sleep for thinking of him. Let's go and look for him ourselves."

So they took their boat and sculled quietly up the river, as the sun came up and the birds began to twitter. Everything smelled fresh and green.

They went further up the river than they had ever been before, and came to a little island.

"Listen!" said Ratty, shipping his oars. "Do you hear music?" Mole rowed closer. He could not hear anything. Ratty's eyes were shining. He seemed very far away, as if he were under a spell.

"Go closer!" said Ratty. They moored their boat and made their way through the reeds to the grassy bank. Now Mole could hear the music, too.

It was piping, very high and clear. It seemed to draw the two animals towards a little clearing under the trees. They felt as if they were in some holy place.

Then they saw the Protector of all animals, sitting under a tree, with the Pan pipes in his hand. They saw his horns and his strong, kind face, brown chest and shaggy goat limbs. Nestled between his hooves slept the podgy childish form of the baby otter.

For one second the little animals saw this

vision, and heard the music. Then suddenly it was gone, and the glade was empty. The baby otter awoke and with whimpering cries searched the clearing for its lost friend.

Mole and Ratty took Portly back with them to the ford where the Otter waited so patiently. From a little way off, they watched the happy meeting. Then they went home, wondering, and feeling that something very special had happened to them that day. But they could not remember it.

8 The Further Adventures of Toad

Toad was getting nearer and nearer to home, and still had on his washerwoman's disguise. (By now it was looking the worse for wear.) Presently he came to a tow-path, running alongside a canal. An old horse was plodding along it, pulling a gaily painted barge. A big stout woman sat in it, her brawny arm along the tiller.

Toad saw the chance of a lift, so he told his tale of losing a purse and having to get back to the children. "I'll give you a lift as far as Toad Hall," the barge-woman bargained, "if you'll do my dirty washing for me." Toad had been boasting what a good washer-woman he was!

The barge-woman gave him a great pile of washing, some soap and clean water in a big tub. Toad had no idea how to set about it. Soon he was puffing and blowing and rubbing and dubbing, but the clothes were no cleaner.

The barge-woman took a closer look at him.

''You're no washerwoman!'' she shrieked. ''You're a dirty ugly toad — get off my nice clean barge!''

Toad was so annoyed he jumped off the barge, undid the tow-rope, and rode off on the horse, leaving the barge-woman shaking her fist at him.

He galloped along, thinking how clever he was. By now he was feeling hungry, and as he passed a hedge, the most delicious smell came floating over it. A gipsy was cooking a stew of rabbit, pheasant and onions, in an iron pot on a fire. Quickly Toad struck a bargain. He sold the horse, in exchange for a few pence and a plate of stew.

He was feeling his old self again and began to make up a boastful song about his adventures. While he was singing,

> *"The world has held great heroes,*
> *As history books have showed,*
> *But never a name to go down to fame*
> *Compared to Mr Toad —"*

a familiar noise was heard.

Along the highway came a motor-car, and it was the very one Toad had stolen!

Toad pretended to faint and the car stopped. The passengers took him to be a poor washerwoman and put him in the front seat, where the fresh air would revive him. It was not long before Toad perked up enough to ask a favour.

"I've always wanted to see if I could drive a motor-car," he said longingly. "Please let me try!"

The passengers were very amused to think of a humble washerwoman wanting to drive. "Let her have a go!" they said to the chauffeur.

Toad drove off, slowly at first, then faster and faster!

"Be careful, washerwoman!" they cried.

"I'm not a washerwoman!" said he. "I'm the great, the famous Toad!" and he drove faster than ever, terrifying the passengers, until he took a corner too fast and drove straight into a pond.

He jumped out and hopped off across the fields, singing another verse of his boastful song, leaving the passengers standing up to their waists in muddy water.

> *"The clever men at Oxford*
> *Know all that is to be knowed*
> *But none of them knows half as much*
> *As intelligent Mr Toad!"*

But when he looked back he saw the chauffeur and two policemen running after him.

41

Poor Toad puffed along. He was a very fat animal and they were gaining on him. What a fool he had been, showing off like that! Suddenly he tripped up. He had come to the River Bank, and — splash! — he fell into the water.

He swam along, gasping, till he came to a hole in the bank. He clutched the edge and looked in.

A small, bright thing shone and moved towards him. A face grew up around it.

Brown and small, with whiskers.

Grave and round, with neat ears.

It was the Water Rat!

9 The Battle for Toad Hall

When Toad had been dried off and given a suit of Ratty's to wear, Rat told him what had happened while he had been away.

The Wild Wooders had taken over Toad Hall. Weasels, ferrets and stoats were living there, eating Toad's food and drinking his drink and telling everybody he was never coming back.

Toad was all for going up there at once and turning them out. But Ratty explained that they had armed sentries posted and all the entrances were guarded. He and Badger and Mole patrolled the Hall every day, and there was no way in.

Just then two tired, shabby animals entered. The Badger's clothes were covered with mud.

He said solemnly: "Welcome home, Toad. Alas, what am I saying? This is a poor homecoming. Unhappy Toad." And he sat down and cut himself a piece of cold pie.

But Mole, whose fur was full of bits of hay and straw, danced round Toad joyously and said: "You must have escaped! O *clever* Toad!"

At this, Toad began to tell all his adventures and show off to the admiring Mole.

"Don't egg him on, Mole," said Ratty. "We have to think what to do next."

They all began to talk at once, until they were silenced by the Badger.

"Be quiet, all of you," he growled. He finished his pie and had a piece of cheese before he spoke again.

"Toad, you bad, troublesome little animal! Aren't you ashamed of yourself? What do you think your father, my old friend, would have said if he'd known of your goings-on?"

The Toad rolled over on his face on the sofa and began to sob.

"Never mind that!" said Badger. "We'll let bygones be bygones. I'll tell you my plan to get Toad Hall back again. There is an underground passage — '' And the Badger outlined his plan to the eager listeners.

The secret passage came up inside Toad Hall, in the butler's pantry, next to the banqueting hall. That night there was to be a birthday party for the Chief Weasel. Everyone would be in the banqueting hall having a good time, except for a few sentries outside in the grounds.

Badger and his men would creep along the tunnel, armed to the teeth, then come up inside the Hall and take the Wild Wooders by surprise.

Badger had a pile of weapons, and Ratty distributed them into four little heaps. As he ran from one to the other, he muttered busily, ''Here's a sword for the Rat, here's a sword for the Mole, here's a sword for the Toad, here's a sword for the Badger! Here's a pistol for the Rat, here's a pistol for the Mole — '' and so on, till all the weapons were sorted out.

Then they had a supper of baked beans and macaroni cheese. When it was dark, they put on their belts and their pistols and swords, and set off for the secret passage. Badger led the way, flourishing a thick stick.

They kept stopping in the darkness, and bumped into each other several times. This gave Toad, who was last, quite a fright. But soon they could hear the noise of the feast, overhead — the stamping of little feet, clinking of glasses, and cheers.

"Now, boys, all together!" said Badger, and they heaved at the trapdoor. They came up into the butler's pantry, and could hear the Chief Weasel giving a speech of thanks.

"I should like to say a word about our kind host, Mr Toad," he sniggered. "*Good* Toad! *Modest* Toad! *Honest* Toad!"

Everybody laughed. "In return for his hospitality, I have made up a little song about him!"

Then the Chief Weasel began to sing a very rude song, all about motor-cars and prison, at the top of his squeaky little voice.

"Let me get at him!" said Toad.

"NOW!" cried the Badger, and they burst into the banqueting hall, laying about them with their weapons.

My!

What a squeaking and a squealing and a screeching filled the air!

Terrified weasels dived under the tables.
Ferrets rushed madly for the fireplace, and got
hopelessly stuck in the chimney.

The mighty Badger laid about him with his
stick. Mole gave a terrible war cry, "A Mole!
A Mole!" Rat flourished his pistol. Toad,
swollen to twice his usual size, went straight
for the Chief Weasel. There were only the four
of them, but to the Wild Wooders they seemed
like an army.

At last the room was clear, and all the
weasels fled squeaking back to the Wild
Wood, except for a few Mole had given
brooms and aprons, and set to tidy up the
Hall.

10 The Wanderer's Return

Next day Toad wanted to give a banquet for his friends and neighbours to celebrate his homecoming. He spent the morning making out a programme, full of Songs (by Toad), and Speeches (by Toad), on subjects like "Our Prison System" and "Horse-dealing".

When his friends saw it they told him what they thought of him. "You *must* turn over a new leaf, Toad," they said, "and stop showing off!"

"No speeches?"

"No speeches!"

"Not one little song?"

"Not *one* little song!"

Poor Toad! He had to promise to reform.
But up in his bedroom, looking in the mirror,
he sang his last little song in praise of himself.
It was called '' When the Toad Came Home.''

The Toad – came – home!
There was panic in the parlour
and howling in the hall,
There was crying in the cowshed
and shrieking in the stall,
When the Toad – came – home!

When the Toad – came – home!
There was smashing in of window
and crashing in of door,
There was chivvying of weasels
that fainted on the floor,
When the Toad – came – home!

Bang! go the drums!
The trumpeters are tooting
and the soldiers are saluting,
And the cannon they are shooting
and the motor-cars are hooting,
As the Hero comes!

Shout – Hoo – ray!
And let each one of the crowd
try and shout it very loud,
In honour of an animal
of whom you're justly proud,
For it's Toad's – great – day!

Toad sang this very loudly, with expression, and when he came to the end, he sang it all over again. Then he went quietly downstairs to greet his guests. He refused to take any credit for the victory. "No, no, it was all Badger's idea. Mole and Rat did most of the fighting," he said modestly. Mole and Rat looked at each other. This was indeed an altered Toad!

The gaoler's daughter and the engine driver were sent letters of thanks and presents. The barge-woman was sent the value of her horse, though Toad protested. The gipsy was sent nothing, as he had done rather well out of the deal.

The four friends sometimes took a stroll together in the Wild Wood of a summer evening. Respectful mother weasels pointed them out to the young ones, and told them to behave, or the terrible great grey Badger would get them. This was somewhat unfair to Badger, who was fond of children. But it never failed to make them behave.

THE END

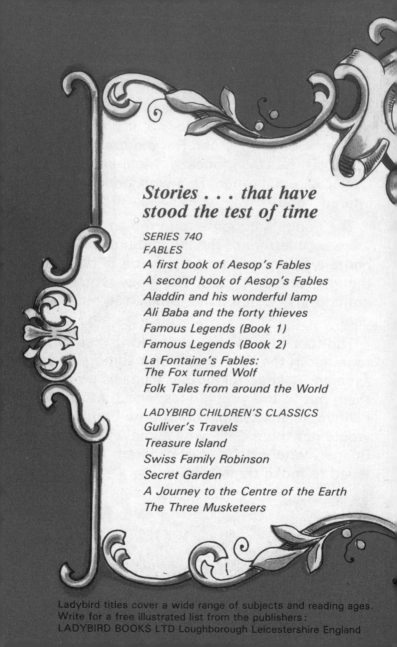

Stories . . . that have stood the test of time

SERIES 740
FABLES
A first book of Aesop's Fables
A second book of Aesop's Fables
Aladdin and his wonderful lamp
Ali Baba and the forty thieves
Famous Legends (Book 1)
Famous Legends (Book 2)
La Fontaine's Fables:
The Fox turned Wolf
Folk Tales from around the World

LADYBIRD CHILDREN'S CLASSICS
Gulliver's Travels
Treasure Island
Swiss Family Robinson
Secret Garden
A Journey to the Centre of the Earth
The Three Musketeers

Ladybird titles cover a wide range of subjects and reading ages.
Write for a free illustrated list from the publishers:
LADYBIRD BOOKS LTD Loughborough Leicestershire England